WITHDRAWN
PROPERTY OF:
DAVID O. McKAY LIBRARY
MAR 28 2024
BYU-IDAHO
REXBURG ID 83460-0405
DAVID O. McKAY LIBRARY
BYU-IDAHO

The Pond God and other stories

The Pond God and other stories

Samuel Jay Keyser

DRAWINGS BY
Robert Shetterly

FRONT STREET
Asheville, North Carolina

Designed by Helen Robinson
Printed in the United States

First edition

Library of Congress Cataloging-in-Publication Data
Keyser, Samuel Jay
The pond god and other stories / Samuel Jay Keyser;
drawings by Robert Shetterly.
p. m.
Summary: A collection of original tales inspired by a Navajo shaman and featuring a variety of "gods".
ISBN 1-886910-96-0
1. Fables, American 2. Children's stories, American.
[1. Fables.] I. Shetterly, Robert, ill. II. Title.
PZ8. 2. K46Po 2003 [Fic]—dc21

The stories in this volume were inspired by
a Navajo shaman who once said that he had seen
a god walking across the horizon.
The horizon is not a place but a perspective.
What happens there depends on who you are.

These stories are dedicated to Nancy Kelly,
who brought them to me,
and to Hilary Goodman,
who brought them to you.

Contents

Contents

The Pond God and other stories

1 The Pond God

A young god could take any shape he wished.
Once he changed into a bee and stung the other gods.
Infuriated, they chased him across the horizon.
He changed into a lake, but the gods each took
a single mouthful and left him to be a pond forever.

Time passed. A forest grew. Through its trees
his watery eyes reflected the blue sky and the stars.
Dead leaves floated over his rippled forehead.
Clouds, slow in summer, faster in winter,
drifted across his cheeks, wrinkled by the wind.
Fish and frogs, lily pads and water snakes
grew inside his belly.
In winter, when they died, he was locked in grief.
In spring, when they thrived, tears of joy swelled him.

A thousand years passed, and the gods, taking pity,
went to the pond and spat out their mouthfuls.
The pond became a lake, but the god did not reappear.

Why do you not rejoin us? asked the gods.

Because, replied the lake, I am content not to.

And that is why contentment is not something one seeks
but something one finds.

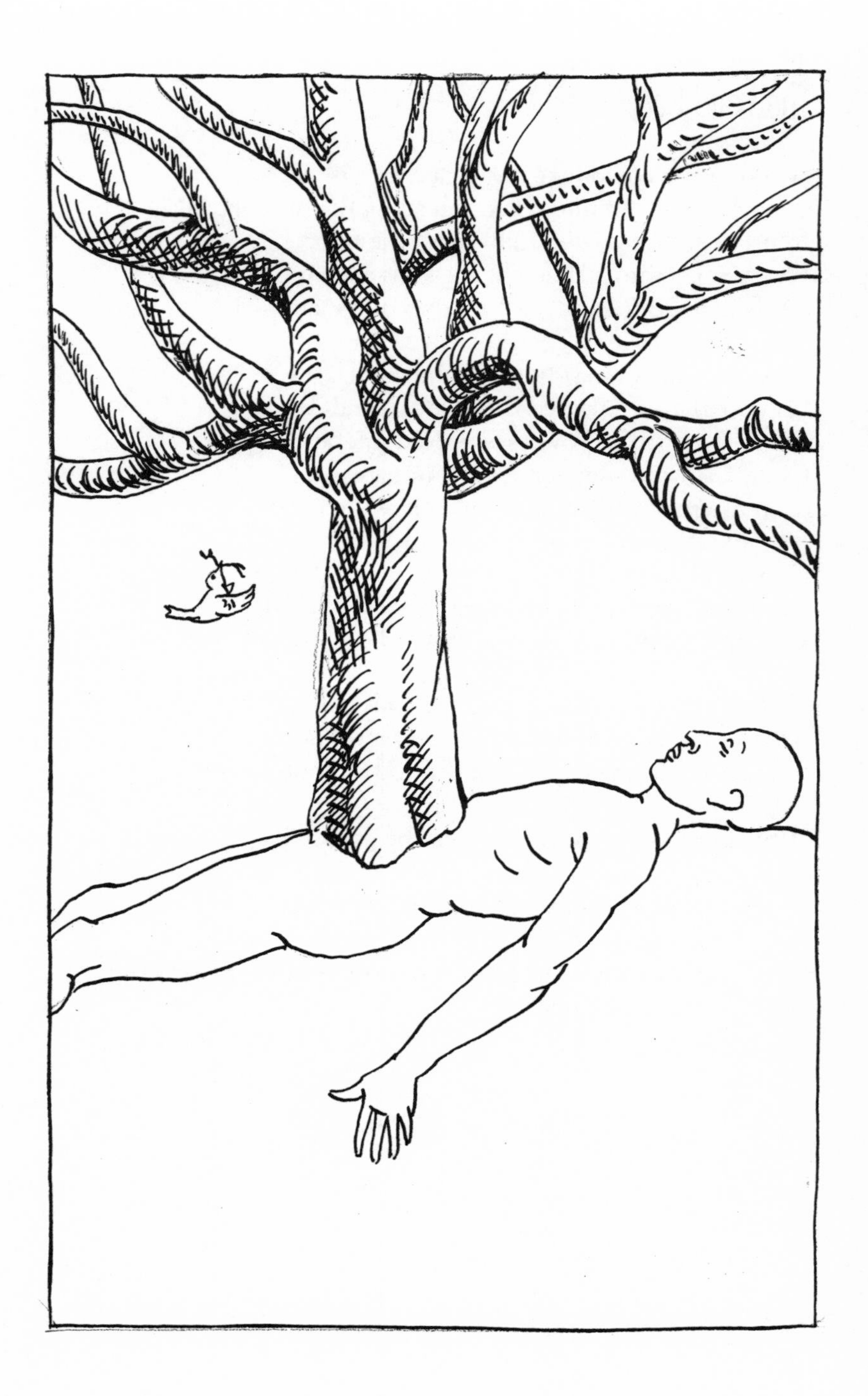

How a God Lost Himself and Found Beauty

Once a god swallowed an acorn.
He had been sleeping beneath an oak when a lark began
to sing. The song was beautiful and he sat up to listen,
but the startled bird flew off, dislodging an acorn.

Come back, cried the god.
That was when he swallowed it.

The acorn took root.
The tree grew bigger until it pressed him to the earth,
and when its branches pierced his navel,
he could not move.

Another god said, I'll cut down your tree.
Then you will walk again.

If you kill the tree, the god replied,
I will die as well.

So he lay for ten thousand days,
until one morning a lark began to build a nest in his branches,
singing a song more beautiful than he had ever heard.
Now, when the lark sang,
the god kept the branches of his tree perfectly still.

And that is how a lark found peace
and a god surrendered to beauty.

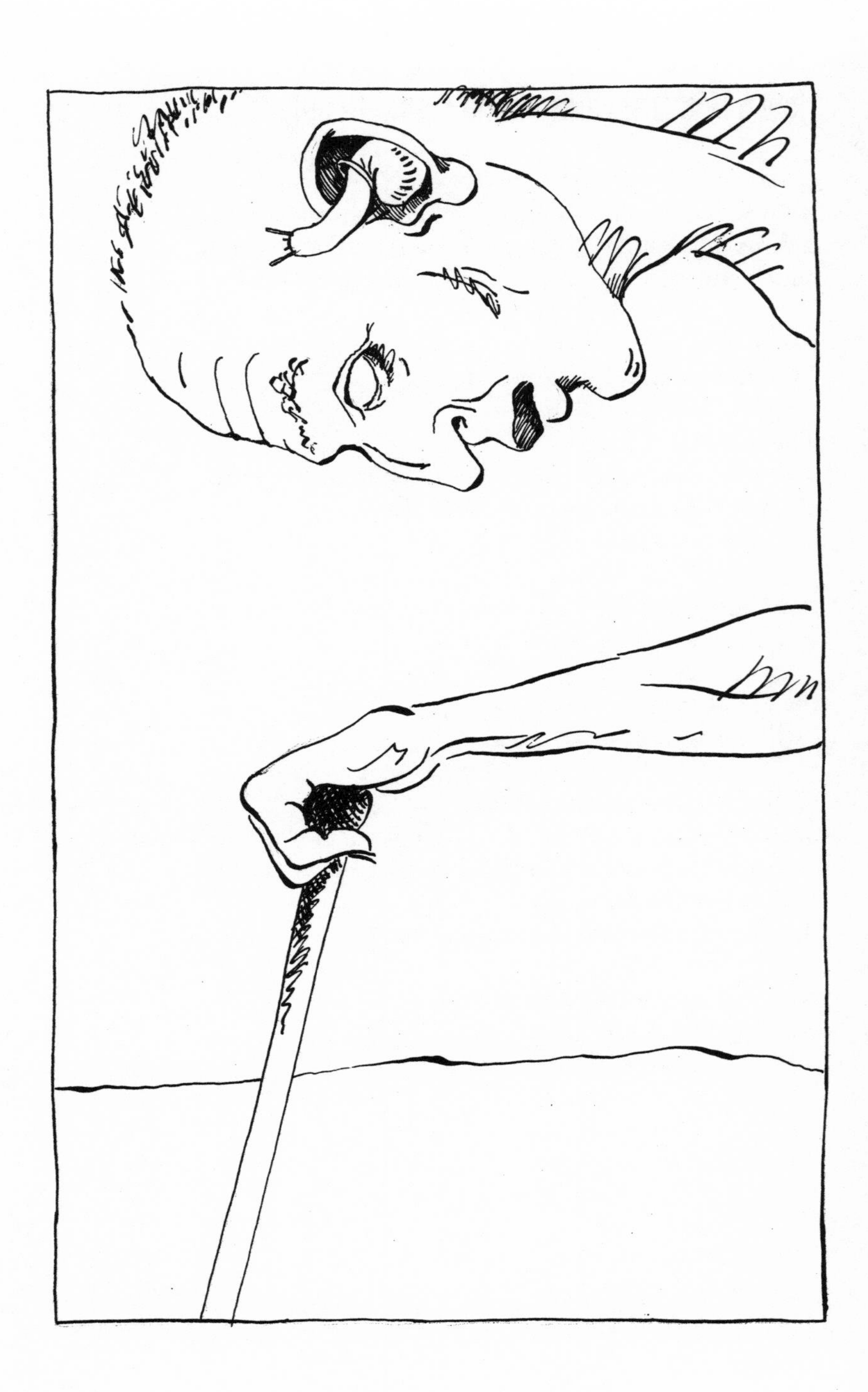

3 | The Crooked God

Once a god's back was so bent,
he stared at his feet when he walked.
To see to either side, he shook his head.
To see ahead, he lay on his back.

He seemed so absurd, this shepherd's crook,
the other gods played tricks.
Careful, one would shout. Boulder ahead!
The crooked god would turn sideways
only to see the other gods laughing.

One day, as he walked along the horizon,
he stepped over a snail
crossing his path.

Let me repay you for not treading on me, said the snail.

How can you possibly repay me?

Put me inside your ear and you shall see.

No sooner was the snail inside the crooked god's ear
than a god cried,
Watch out! Tree ahead.

Pay no attention, said the snail.

The way is clear, offered another god
as the crooked god walked toward a thicket.

Step to the left, whispered the snail,
or you will snag yourself on a thorn bush.

From that day on, the crooked god walked as if he were upright,
and before long the gods forgot that he was crooked.

And that is how two can change what one cannot.

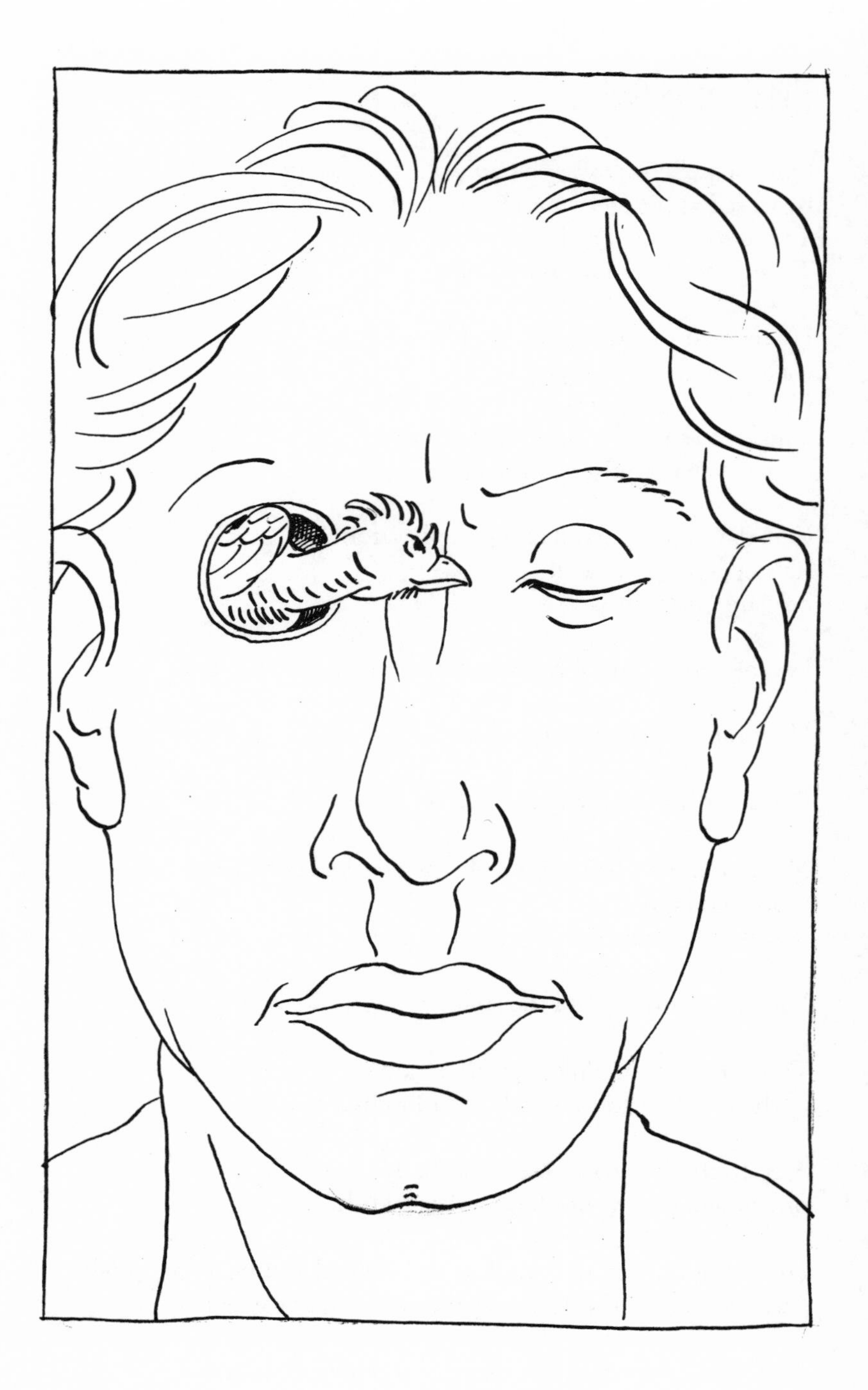

How a Bird Went Free

Once a god was dozing under a tree
when a bird lit on his forehead.
Thinking his eyebrow was a worm,
the bird started to peck at it
just as the unwary god opened one eye.

The bird pecked it out.

You have swallowed my eye!
cried the angry god, grabbing the bird.
Now I will swallow you.

I meant no harm, peeped the tiny bird.

Perhaps. But you have harmed me all the same
and now you must pay.

How can I pay for an eye? asked the bird.

Sit where my eye used to be
and tell me everything you see,
said the god.

For ten thousand days the bird sat in the empty socket,
telling the god what lay ahead.
The bird was so dutiful that the god grew lazy
and kept his good eye shut.
Soon his eyelids grew together.
When the bird realized what had happened, she flew away,
leaving the god alone and blind.

And that is why it is better to trust one eye that is your own
than two that are another's.

5 | How a Thief Stole the Horizon

In the beginning, when it was always dark,
a god plucked out the eye of a giant fish
and hung it in the sky. Night became day,
and the place between the water and the sky
was where the gods began to walk.

One day while the thieving god walked along the horizon,
a fish jumped out of a breaking wave and swallowed him.

Why have you done this? said the god from the fish's belly.

Because you stole my eye, said the fish.

If I give it back, will you let me go?

How do I know you won't run away?

I promise, and a god's promise can never be broken.

So the fish set the god back on the shore.
But when he did, the god plucked out the fish's other eye
and hung it in the sky to look down on the Earth at night.

And that is how some say the sun and moon came to be
and why it is better to live with one eye than bargain with a thief.

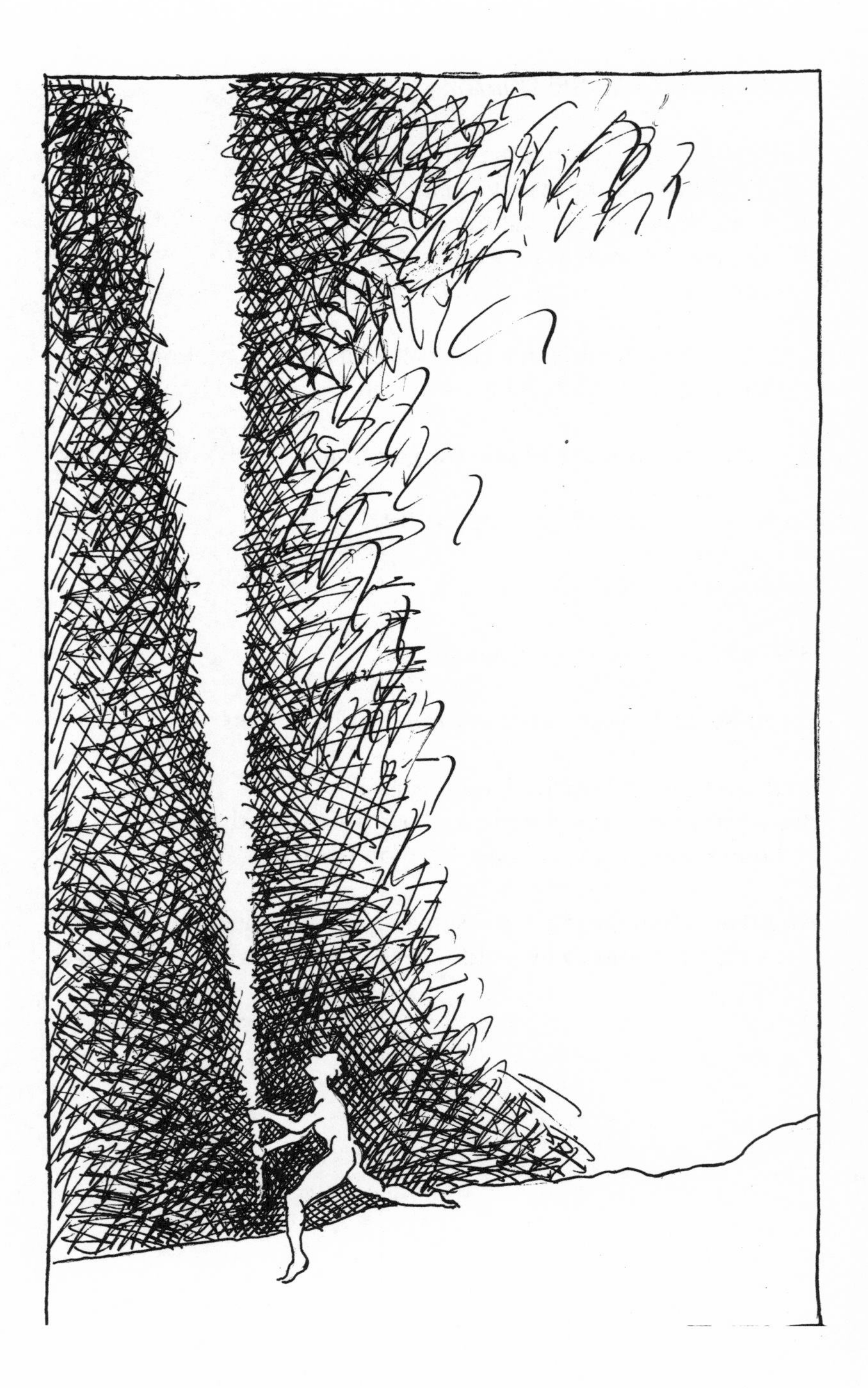

How the Sun Tricked a God

One day the sun dropped a shaft of light at the foot of a god,
who picked it up and carried it away.

Where are you going with that shaft of light? asked the sun.

To weave a cloak, the god answered.

But if you weave a cloak from my light,
the world will stay in darkness.

Perhaps, but I found it. It is mine to do with as I please.

So the god wove a cloak for his shoulders,
and wherever he went, it was day.
Wherever he was not, it was night.

The sun, who was determined to get back his light,
disguised himself as an old man
and sat along the horizon to wait for the thieving god.

When the god came walking by, the old man started to shiver.
I am so cold, he said.
If you let me warm myself in your cloak,
I will show you where the moon keeps her light.

The god agreed,
but the moment the cloak touched his shoulders,
the sun rose into the sky and began to shine again.

And that is how it takes a thief to catch one.

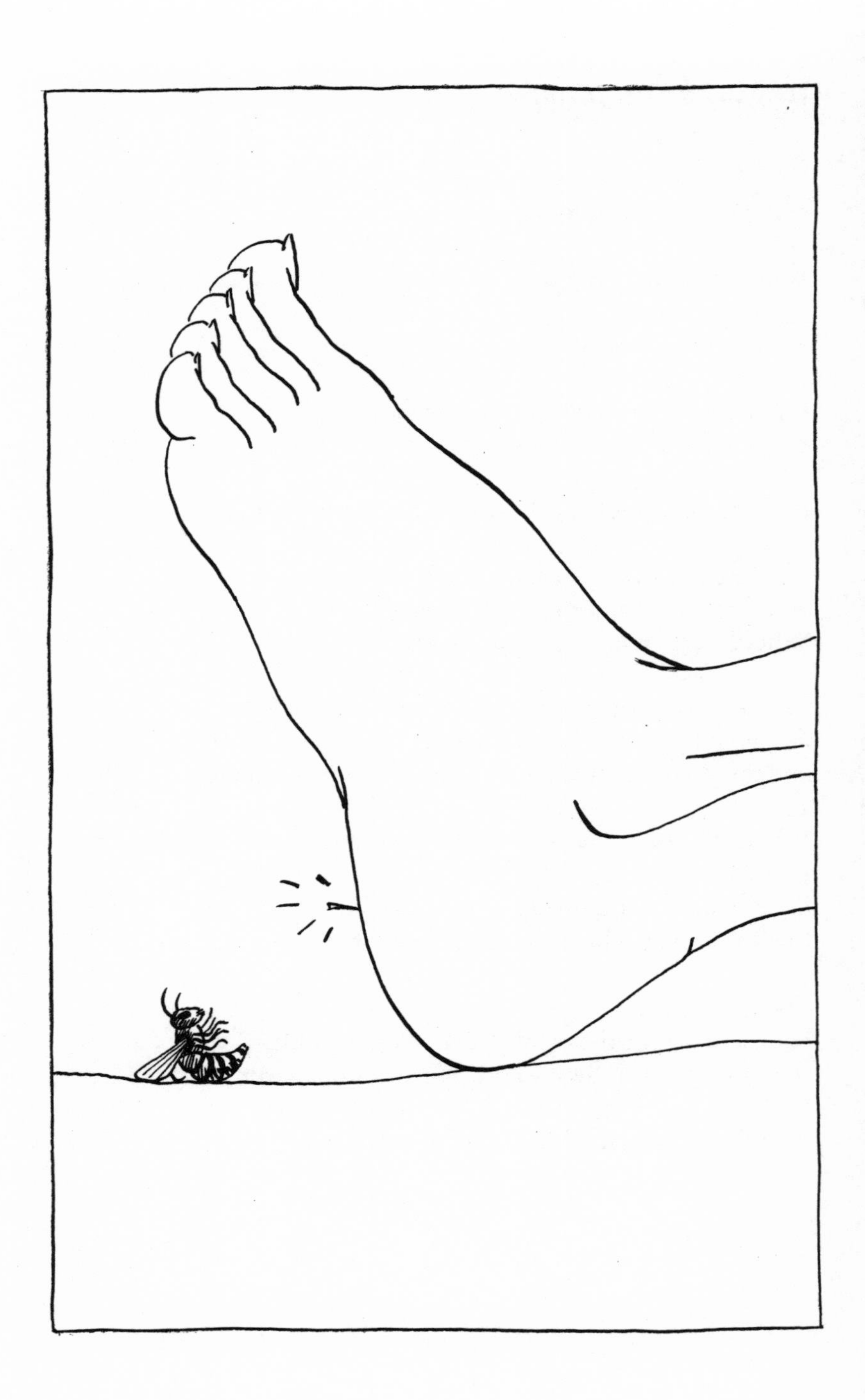

7 | How a God Hid Behind the Wind

Once a god sat beside a pool and watched as the wind blew
clouds, birds, drops of rain across the sky
so that their reflection mingled with her own.
One day a bee the size of her thumb thrust its stinger
deep into the god's heel.

Why did you sting me? she cried.

I had no choice, said the bee, dying at her foot.
The wind blew me against you, and it is in my nature to sting.

The god drew the stinger out of her heel.

You are a god, said the bee.
If you give me back my stinger, I will not die.

But you will sting me again.

It is in my nature, said the bee with a shrug.

The god placed the stinger on one leaf, the bee on another,
and set them afloat on the surface of the pool.

Why are you doing this? asked the bee.

The wind decided before, said the god. Let it decide again.

The God and the Spider

Once a god sat on the horizon,
watching a spider big as a coconut spin a web in a palm tree.
Suddenly the wind tore through the web,
blowing the spider to the ground.

If you will lift me up into the tree again,
I will spin another web, said the spider.

How do I know you won't bite me? asked the god.

What possible reason could I have for biting you? said the spider.

The god could think of none,
but as she reached down to lift the spider into the tree,
the spider bit her on the thumb.

Spider, cried the god,
why have you bitten me?

Why should I be put out and you left in peace? replied the spider,
scurrying up the tree and out of the god's reach.

And that is how what you don't know can hurt you.

9 | The Flailing God

Once there was a god who flailed his arms,
which were round as barrels.
The other gods kept their distance.
One morning this god sat on the horizon
flailing away like a windmill
when a bird in a nearby tree said,
Stop that commotion. You churn the air like a windstorm.

I cannot, replied the god, breathless.
A giant bee is buzzing around my head.
If I stop, he will surely sting me.

The bird fluttered as close as he dared.
Sure enough, there was a bee as big as the god's thumb
buzzing around his head.

Why do you torment him? asked the bird.

He has stolen honey from my hive, said the bee.
I am going to punish him for his crime.

But if you sting him, you will die yourself.

It doesn't matter. He stole my honey.

You can replenish your honey,
but you cannot replenish your life,
said the bird.

With that the bee flew back to his hive
and left the exhausted god in peace.

And that is how the cost of the punishment
can exceed the cost of the crime.

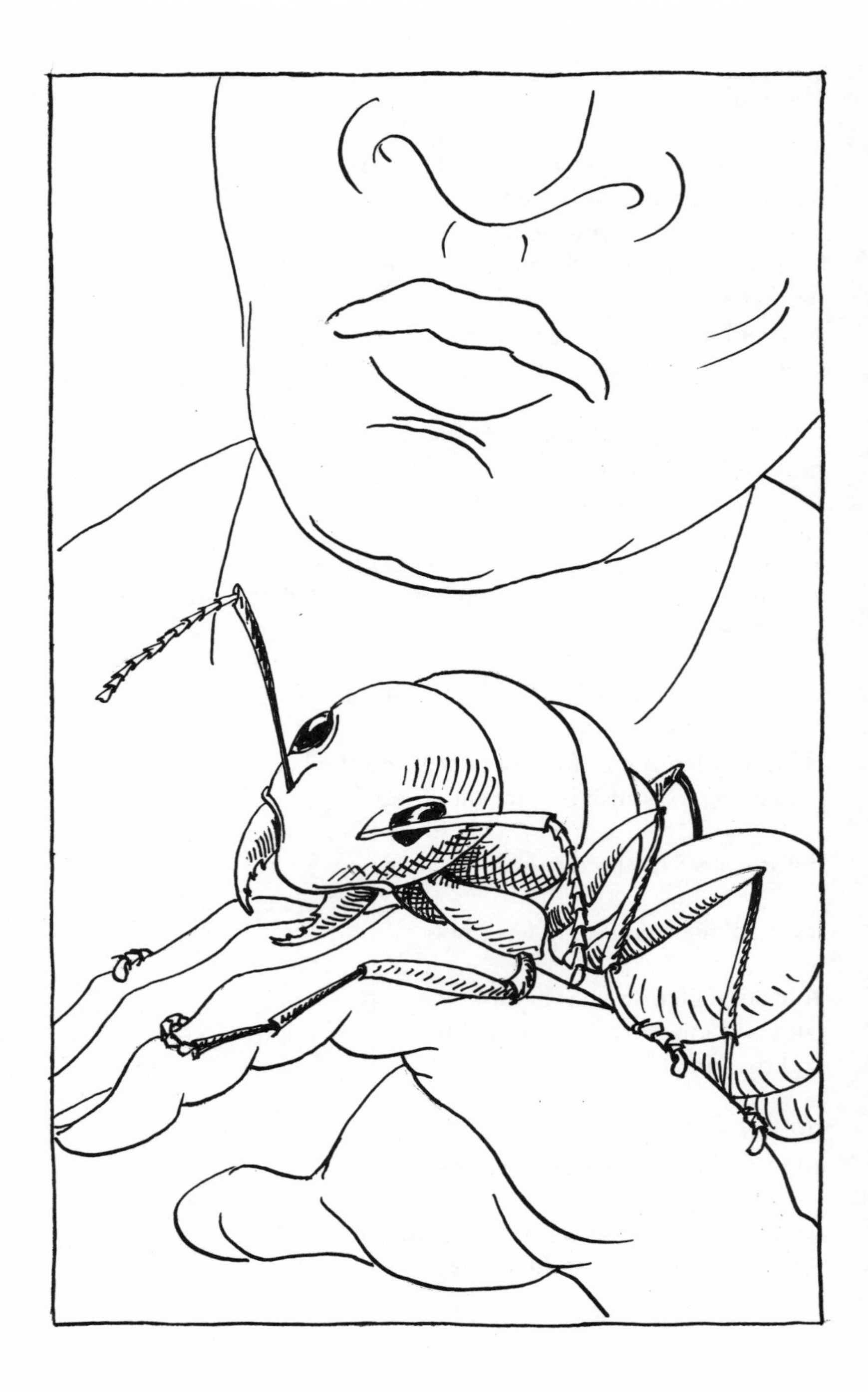

How a God Remained True to His Nature

Once a god fell asleep in a meadow.
When he awoke, he was surrounded by ten thousand ants
brandishing their front legs and hissing like snakes.

Stop, said the god.
Why are you menacing me?
I hope I did you no harm while I was sleeping.

You have done us no harm, said the largest ant.
It is in our nature to ravage.

But, said the god, if you attack me,
I shall grind you into the earth with my heels.

That, said the ant, is neither here nor there.
It is in our nature to attack,
and we have grown accustomed to such treatment
from those we attack.

You are right, said the god.
It would not be in my nature to destroy you,
even though it is in yours to destroy me.

With that the god stepped over the encircling ants
and strode off toward the horizon,
leaving the ants to threaten the air.

And that is why, when given a choice between two natures,
it is best to choose your own.

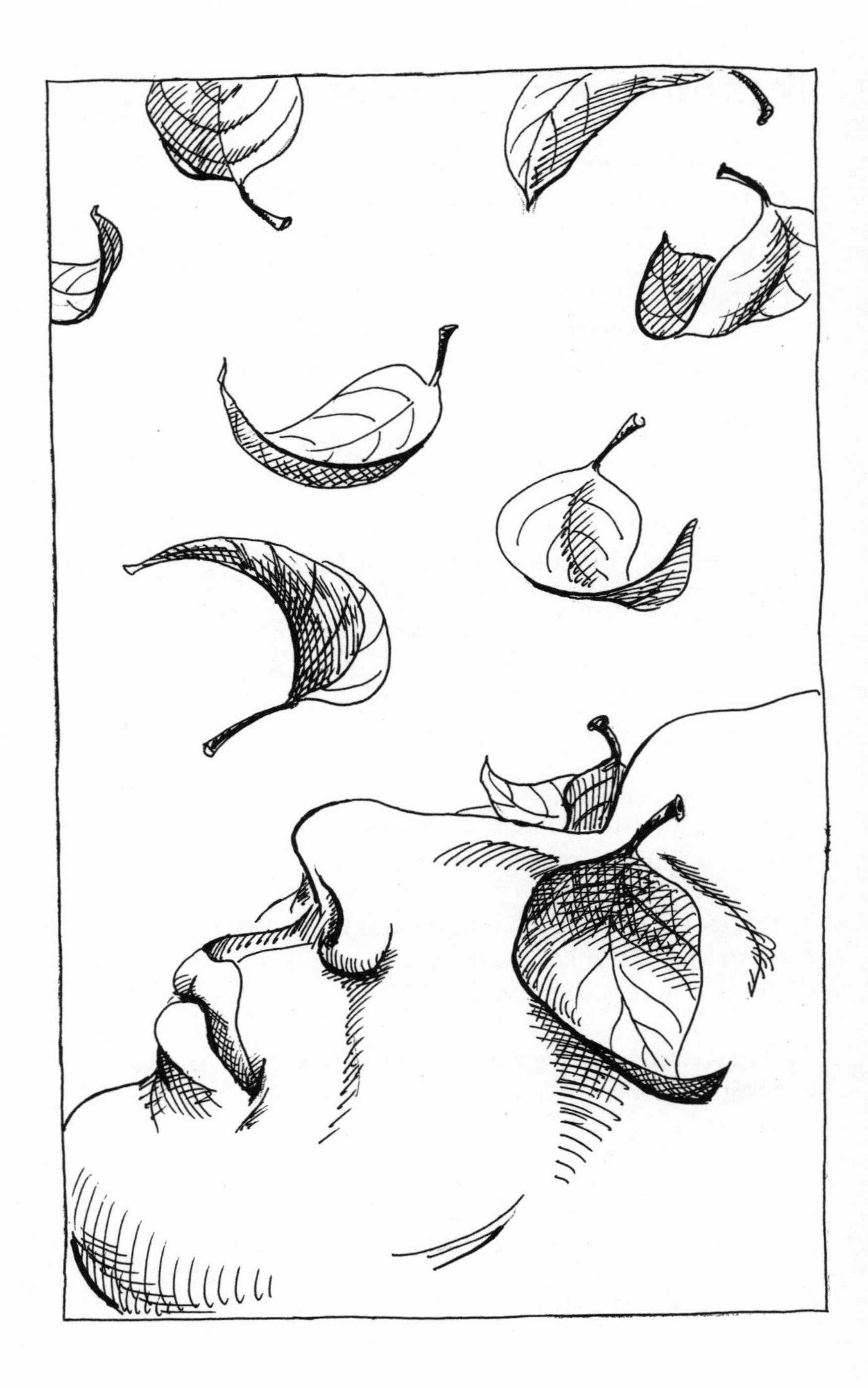

11 How the Gods Learned to Wait

When the gods could not sleep,
they would lay a green leaf over each eye.
The undersides were so soft and cool
that in no time the gods were asleep.
One day a god awoke to find his leaves gone
and, in their stead, a fat locust sitting on each eyelid.
When he opened his eyes wide, the locusts flew off.

Wait! cried the god. You have taken my leaves.

Your leaves? inquired one locust.
How could we know they were yours?

The wind gave them to me, the god replied.

Then ask the wind for more, shouted the other locust.

The god went straight to the wind,
but the wind just shrugged.
The greedy locusts have eaten them all, said the wind.

But what shall we do if there are no green leaves
with soft undersides to soothe us? moaned the god.

I will blow the locusts so far away,
the trees will have time to grow new ones,
promised the wind.

And that is why locusts come once every seventeen years
and why the gods are patient.

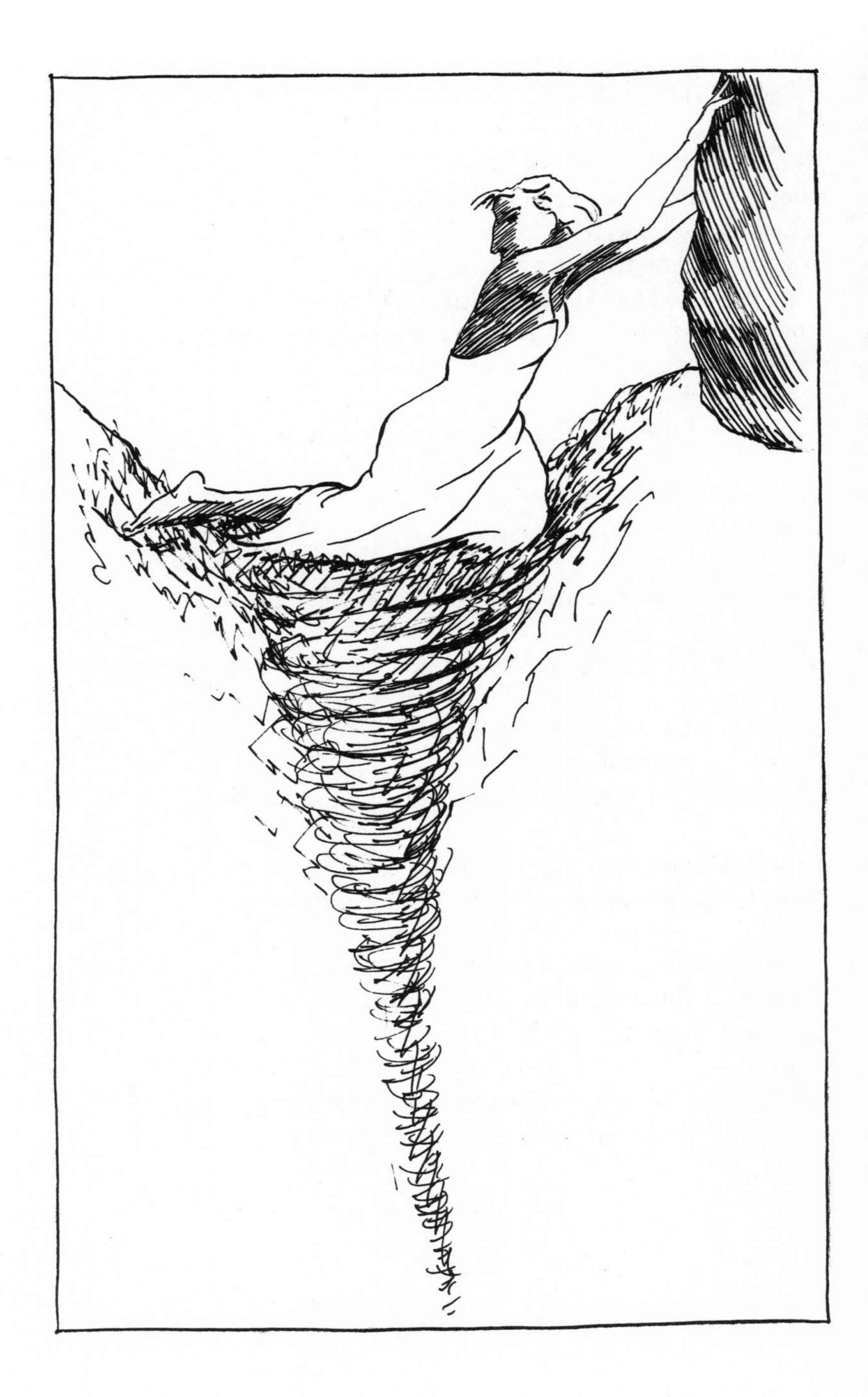

The Pious God

Once there was a god so pious,
the trees swayed when she passed
and the tide ebbed when she went wading.

One day she said to the ground,
The trees and the water show me reverence. You must do the same.

You are right, replied the ground.
I am not worthy even to lie beneath your feet.

And from then on, whenever the god went walking,
the ground gave way beneath her feet
like the side of a sand dune.

I cannot walk when such reverence is shown me,
said the exasperated god.

I show you the reverence you deserve, said the ground.

Show me reverence some other way, demanded the god.

It is the only way I know, replied the ground, giving way again.

The god fell to her knees and crawled to a rock
where she sat, pondering.

Ground, she said, if you show me reverence,
I shall not be able to move from this rock,
and if I cannot move from this rock,
then you will never be able to show me reverence.

Yes, said the ground.

And that is why indifference is sometimes better than respect.

13 | The Old God and the Very Young God

Once there was a god who was so old that the other gods said,
You are a burden to us. Go away.

So the ancient god went where he thought no one would find him.
There he stayed for a thousand years, watching the sun rise and fall.

One day a very young god came walking by.

Hello, said the very young god. Why are you alone?

My companions had no use for me, said the ancient god.

And why is that?

They said I was burdensome.

And why is that?

Because I was so old.

I have just been sent away by my companions.
They said I, too, was a burden.

Why is that? asked the old god.

Because I was too young.

And so they stayed together, as friends do, for the rest of their lives.

And that is how youth and age are burdensome
only to those who have neither.

How the Gods Changed

In the beginning the gods sat on the horizon
with their eyes closed, imagining the world.

One felt a spider build a web against her cheek and said,
Here the wind is made of silk.
It leaves pieces of itself against the face.

Another felt a snake crawl over his outstretched palm.
The air is cold and heavy, he said.
It draws across your skin like a dull knife.

A third felt sand run between his fingers. He said,
The Earth is made of pebbles the size of insects' eyes.
When we walk on it, we will bury ourselves.

A fourth felt the sun at midday and said,
Here time is hot and the minutes are like drops of oil on my brow.

It is time to open our eyes, said a fifth.

The wind is not made of silk, said the first god.
Nor the air weighty, said the second.
The Earth is not made of tiny pebbles, said the third.

They closed their eyes again, but it was not the same.

And that is how the gods could not change the truth
but the truth could change the gods.

15 | How a God Helped a Pigeon

Once a god came upon a pigeon waddling this way and that.
Whichever way the pigeon waddled,
that way went the god.

Why are you following me? asked the pigeon.

I am curious to know what you are looking for, replied the god.

Well, I am looking for food, said the pigeon.

Perhaps I can help, said the god.

Why? asked the pigeon.

Because, said the god, without help you might die.

Thank you, said the pigeon, but I do not need help.

The god went his way and forgot the pigeon until,
one day, he found it
fluttering helplessly on the ground.

I was looking for food when a hawk struck me from behind,
whimpered the pigeon. I think my back is broken.

The god put the pigeon in a cage,
and every morning he went looking for seed
that had fallen along the horizon
to feed the pigeon who could no longer feed itself.

And that is why it is often better to accept help
when one can refuse it than to wait until one cannot.

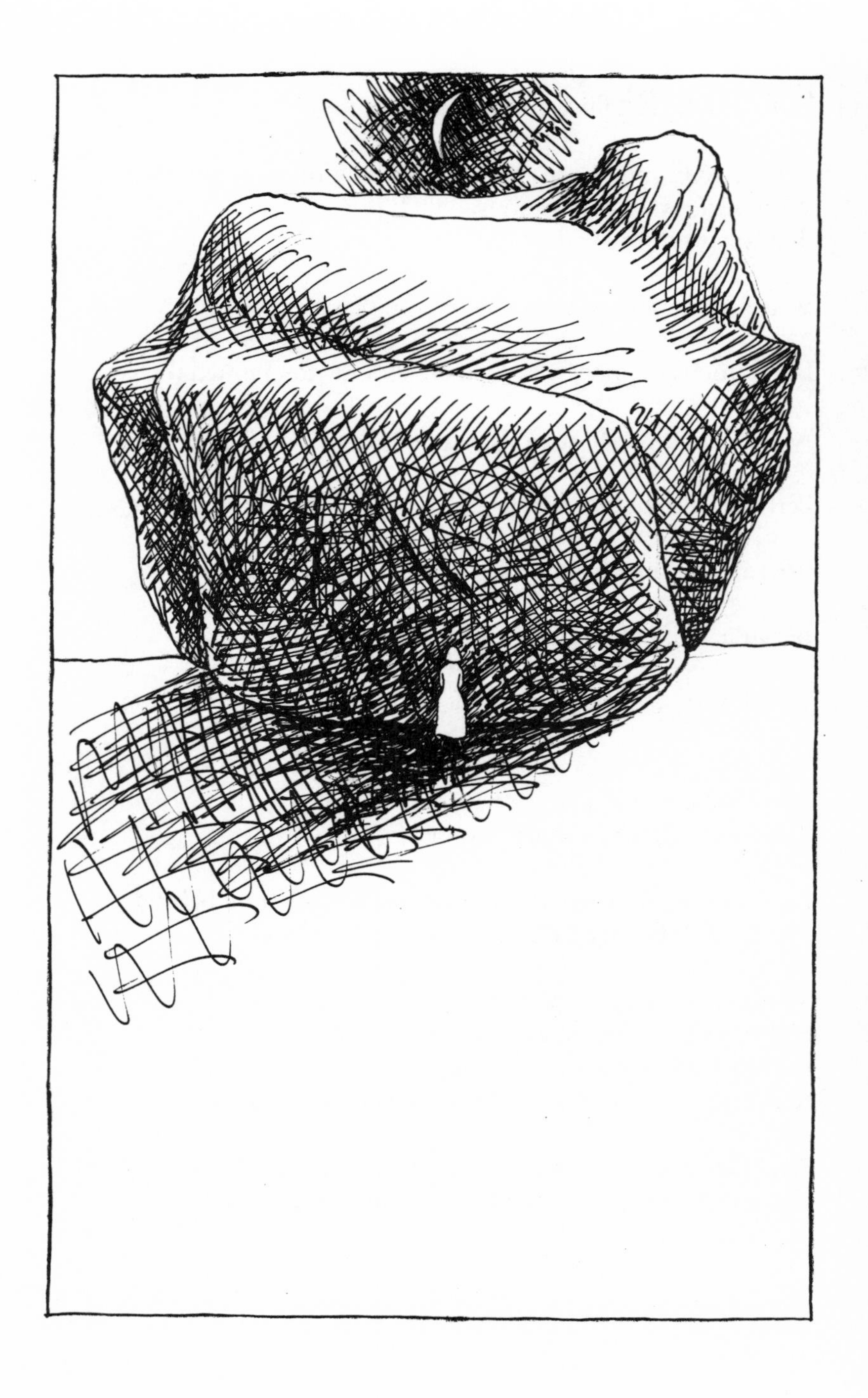

The God Who Walked in Straight Lines

Once there was a god who could walk only in straight lines.
One day as she was walking, a large boulder stood in her way.

Since I cannot go round, she thought,
I shall have to stand here forever.

Just then a god walked by.

Why are you standing in front of that rock? he asked.

The god, ashamed to tell the truth, replied,
Once an ancient god vowed never to sleep
until he reached the horizon.
But the closer he came, the farther it seemed.
Finally, unable to keep his eyes open a moment longer,
he fell asleep in his tracks and turned to stone.
This rock is that old man, and I am paying my respects.

Let me join you, said the other god.

The two of them stood in silence before the rock
until they turned to stone as well.

And that is how two can share a fate only one deserves.

17 | The God with Ears Big as Sails

When the Earth was silent,
a god with ears big as sails walked across the horizon,
listening to the only sound there was,
the beating of his own heart.
Birds had not yet learned to sing.
The waters of the Earth were still.

His heart thumped slowly when he rested,
and when he ran, it sounded like thunder.
Then he would press his hands to his ears,
but that only made the sound grow louder.

I must do something, he told himself.
This thumping in my ears will drive me mad.

And so he roiled the surface of the waters.
He showed the birds how to sing.
He blew the wind across the sky.
Soon the Earth was filled with noise
and the thumping of his heart was drowned in the din.

And that is why the more one hears, the less one hears.

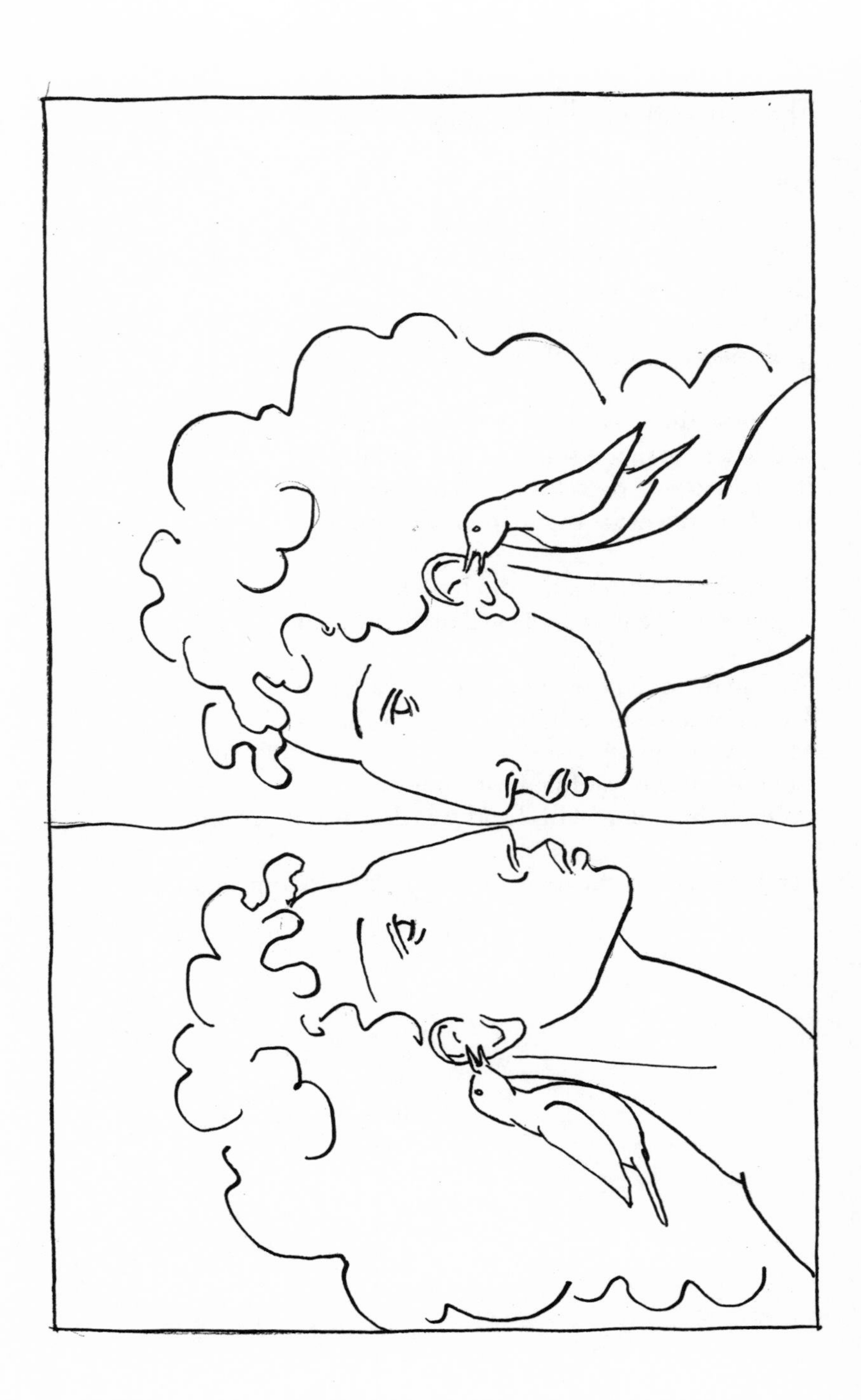

Why the Gods Do Not Speak

Once there was a god who sat on a rock
in the middle of a lake, watching her reflection in the water.
She moved her head from side to side. She raised her arms.
She lowered them. One day a bird sat next to her.
When the god moved, so did the bird.

Why do you do as I do? asked the god.

I am doing as the god in the water does, said the bird.

But why? asked the god.

I will answer when the god in the water asks, said the bird,
flapping his wings just as the god was waving her arms.

There is no god in the water, said the god.
That is my reflection.

Don't be silly, said the bird.
There she is, looking straight at that bird sitting next to her.

Promise me, said the god patiently,
you will do as others do until the god in the water talks to you.

I will promise, said the bird,
if you will promise not to speak until the water god does.

And that is how the mockingbird came to be
and why the gods are silent.

19 May Misfortune Smile on You

Once a god was so thin
you could see through him.
When the wind blew,
he had to hold on
to keep from following the leaves.

One day a god came upon him
blowing from one side of the valley to the other
and grabbed his ankle as he flew by.

Why do you always smile? she asked the thin god.

The thin god replied,
Once there was a god so fat
it took a day for a shiver to make its way
from one side of him to the other.
One day he sat by the roadside panting so hard
rocks began to roll down from the mountainside,
passing first on one side, then on the other,
until they made a wall around him.

What shall I do? he thought
as he tried to push the rocks aside.
I will surely die if I stay here.

And stay there he did,
growing thinner with each day,
until one day he could crawl out between the rocks
and walk along the horizon.

And that is why I smile, said the thin god.

The Willow

Once a god had a sty big as a watermelon on her eyelid.
When she rubbed her eye to make the burning stop,
the sty began to bleed, and when she sat down next to a river
to wash away the blood, the water began to boil.

Can't anyone help me? cried the god in desperation.

A nearby willow tree heard the god.
Quickly, said the willow,
tear off one of my branches
and rub the sap that runs from me over your eyelid.

The god did as the willow said, and soon the sty was gone.
How can I thank you? asked the god.

Can you make my branch grow again? asked the willow.

No, said the god, I cannot.

Can you dull my pain? asked the willow.

No, said the god, I cannot do that either.

Can you protect me from frost, or fall winds,
asked the willow, or the blights of spring and summer?

No, said the god, I can do none of those things.

Then I thank you for the knowledge of pain you have given me,
said the willow.

The god nodded and walked off along the horizon,
leaving the willow tree weeping.

21 The Hideous God

There was a god so hideous
that anyone who looked at him went blind.
One day a rooster caught sight of him.
The hideous god buried his face in his hands,
but it was too late.

Now I cannot see the sun, moaned the rooster.
My master will surely eat me.

Since I am to blame for your blindness, said the hideous god,
I will crow for you.

For a thousand dawns
the hideous god crowed for the rooster
until one morning the master came upon him.

What are you doing? asked the master.

I am crowing for your rooster, he said.
Because of me he is blind.

And why is that? asked the master.

Can't you see I hide my face in my hands? asked the god.
I am so hideous that all who look upon me are blinded.

Well, then, said the master, take your hands from your face.
The rooster crowed for me because I am blind.
Since I have you to crow for me, I shall eat the rooster.

Without a word the god tucked the rooster safely under his arm
and walked off toward the horizon.

And that is how a hideous face can hide a generous heart.

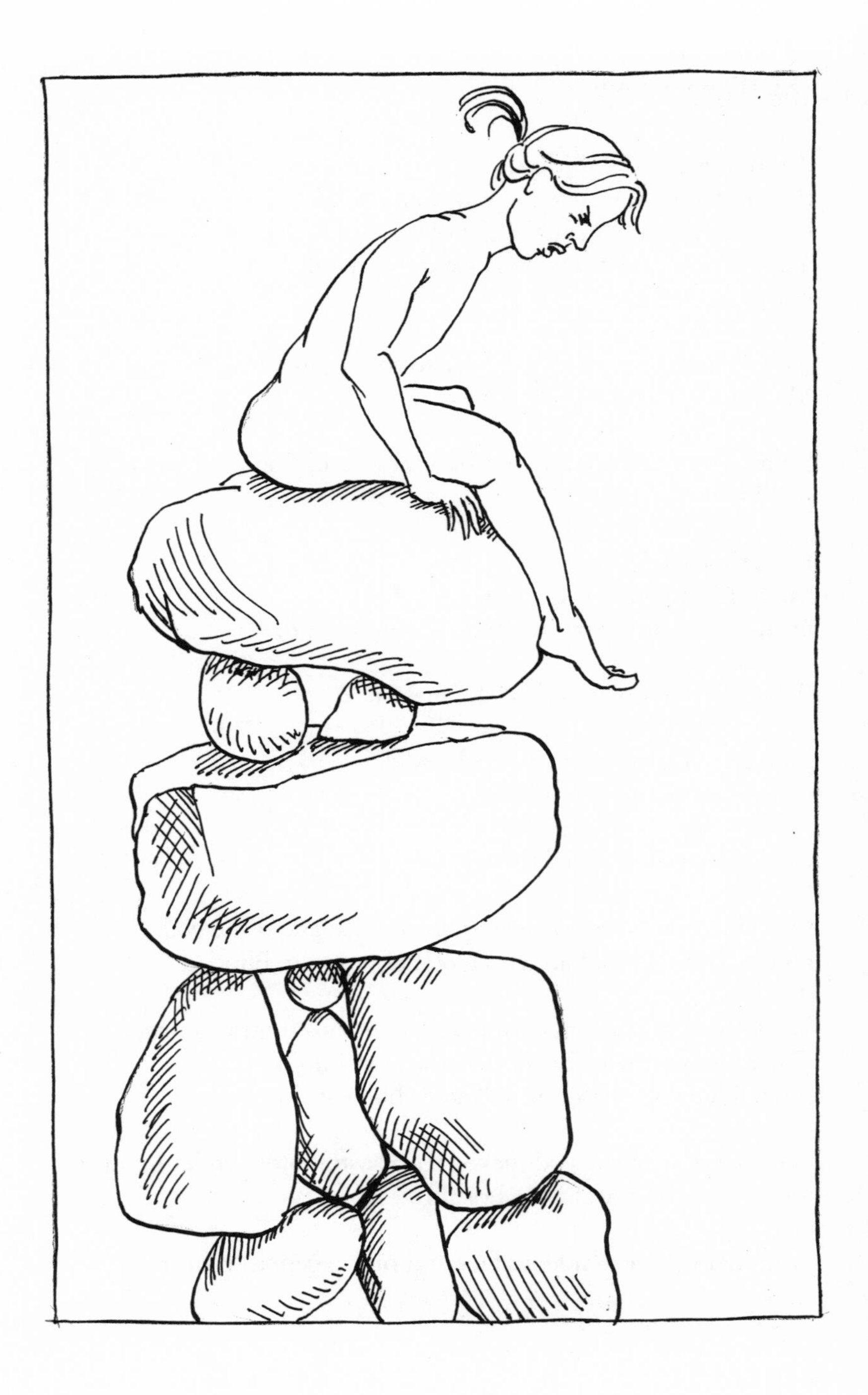

The Magic Sack

When the Earth was still new,
a young god sat on a rock,
spitting obscenities into the wind.
One day an old god hobbled by,
a sack slung over his shoulder.

Hey, old one, spat the young god, why are you so ugly?

Age is not a beautiful thing, replied the old god.
You will see soon enough.

I could never be as ugly as you, snapped the young god.
Instead of carrying that sack, you should wear it over your head.
What's in it, anyway?

My lost youth, the old god answered.

What nonsense, replied the young god,
and she snatched the sack and opened it.

The old god's lost youth jumped out and swallowed
the young god whole, and when he spewed her out again,
she was an old woman, gnarled and wrinkled
like the knot on an ancient tree,
crying salt tears for her own lost youth.

And that is how it is possible to waste one's youth in anger
and spend one's old age in regret.

23 | Where Rain Comes From

Once there was a god who sat crying on the horizon.
No matter how hard he tried,
he could not keep the tears from flowing.

Soon there was a puddle at his feet from all his tears,
then a stream, a lake, a river, an ocean.

You must stop crying, the other gods implored.
If you don't, the world will be flooded by your tears.

I can't help it. I cry because I am sad, said the crying god.

Why are you sad? asked a god.

Because, said the crying god, I have no one to talk to.

But no one talks to you because you are always crying,
explained another god.

So the gods took turns talking to the crying god.
When they did, he would stop crying.
But when they stopped talking,
he would begin to cry all over again.

That is where rain comes from.
Thunder is the sound of the other gods making it stop.

Why Gods Are Like Clouds

When the gods opened their eyes,
they were floating above the horizon
like breath exhaled in winter.

Then the wind blew northward,
and they came to where the sun rose and fell once a year.

Time slows when the wind blows, said a god.

Then the wind blew eastward until a day was a day.

Time races when the wind does, said another.

Then the wind blew southward,
and they came to where they began.

Here time and wind must be the same, said a third god.

Then the wind blew westward
so that it was always night.

When shall we rest? asked a god.

When time stops, said another.

And that is why gods are like clouds
and why, when the air is still, time stops.

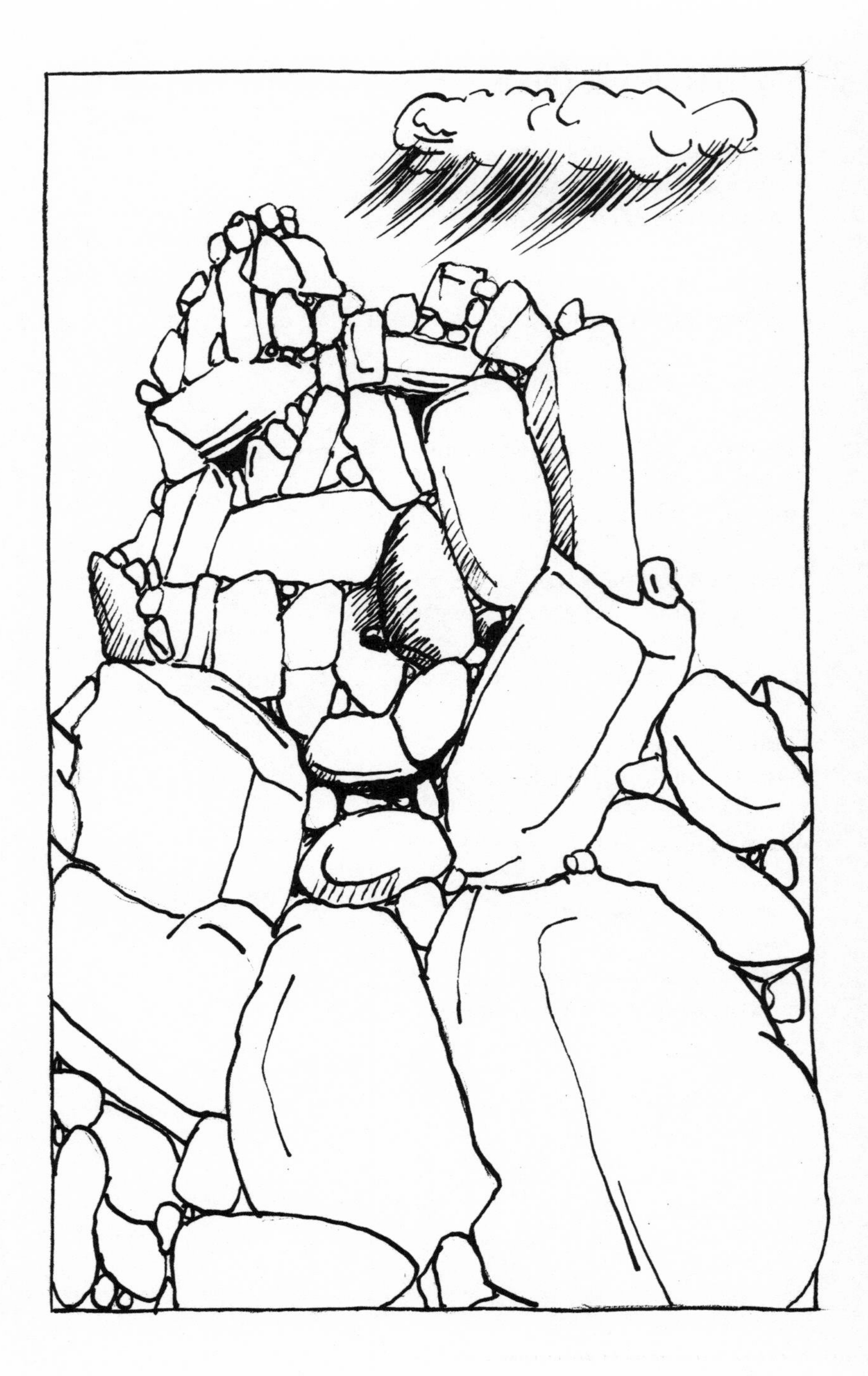

How a God Brought Water to Stones

Where stones lived there were no flowers.
The land was hot and dry.
The wind made devils run, and when the sun set,
the stones stayed hot through the night.

A god, walking along the horizon,
came to where stones lived.
There is nothing for you to drink, the god said.

The dry earth keeps us alive,
the stones replied.

But, said the god,
the cool of water is like wind against your back.
The wet of water is like ointment.
The shape of water is your shape.

Well, then, said the stones,
what must we do for this water?

You must make yourselves into mountains,
the god said.

The stones gathered themselves together and rose
until they touched the water in the sky.
The sound of rain is the sound of stones sighing.

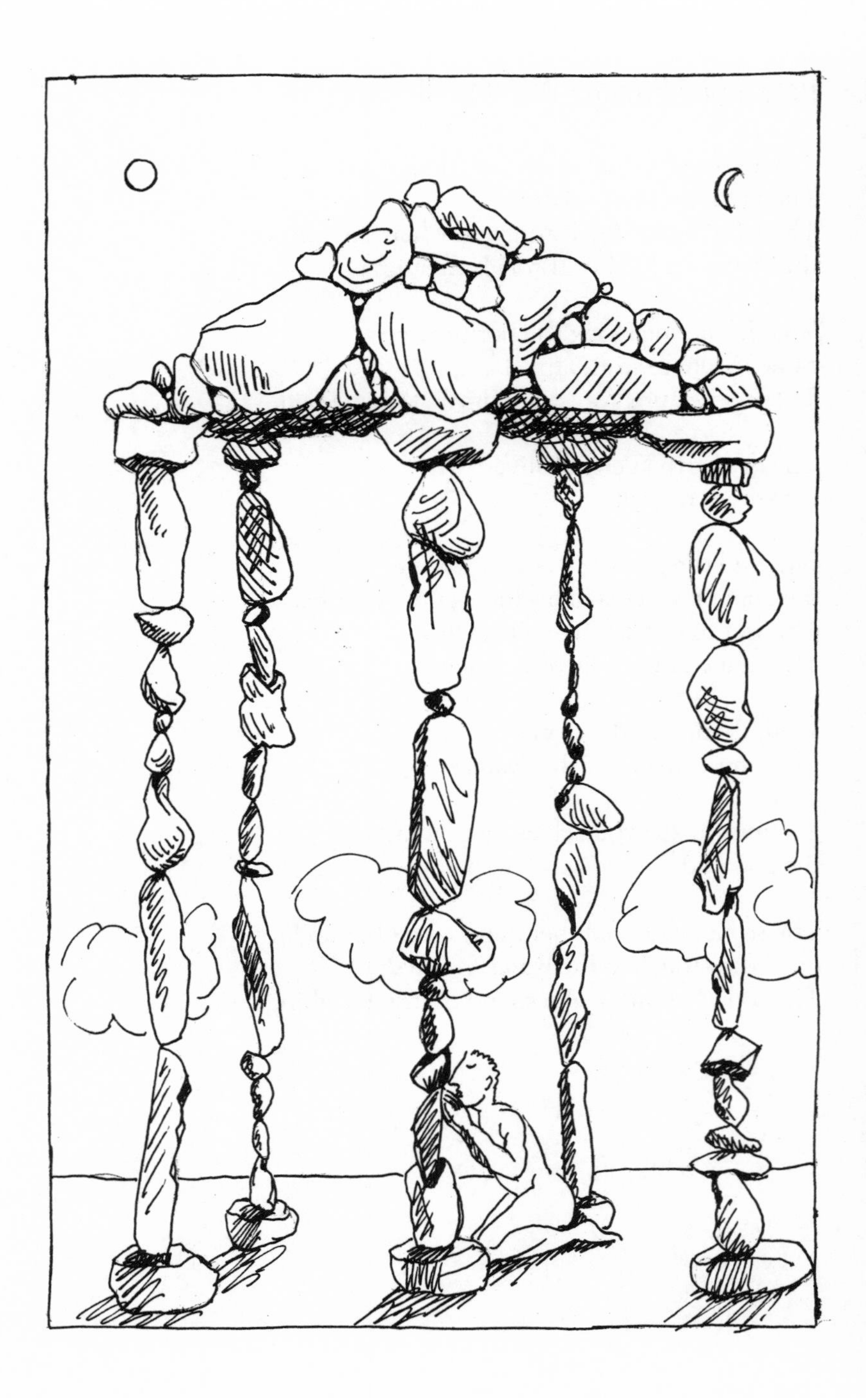

How the Gods Made Altars out of Mountains

One day the gods gathered up stones
that had fallen from the mountains
and built a temple.
When they finished, the first god asked,
Who will pray in this temple?

There is no one but us, said the second.

Then who shall we pray to? asked the third.
It is pointless to pray to ourselves.

Let us make up a god and pray to her, said the fourth.

Where's the good in that? the fifth god said.
It would be like praying to the air.

The sixth god said,
Perhaps it is best to destroy the temple
and return the stones to the mountains.

The mountains were so joyful at the return of their stones
that they caught the wind
and made it whistle through their peaks.

Someday people will hear this, said the seventh god.

And that is why, when we hear the wind
whistling in the mountains,
we think of gods.

27 | Why the Gods Are Invisible

Once a forest of banyan trees grew into the shape of a temple.
It was in the thickest part of the jungle
and so vast that when the gods found it
they floated under its topmost branches
as motes of dust do in the sunlight.

After we have gone from the Earth, people will come, said a god.
They will find this temple and think we were titans.

The other gods joined in.

They will be afraid.

They will bow down and look up when they pray to us.

Though we are no bigger than motes, they will think us giants.

Perhaps we should make ourselves as big as they will imagine us.

No matter how large we make ourselves,
they will make us larger.

It is in their nature, said a god.

And that is why the bigger the gods,
the harder they are to see.

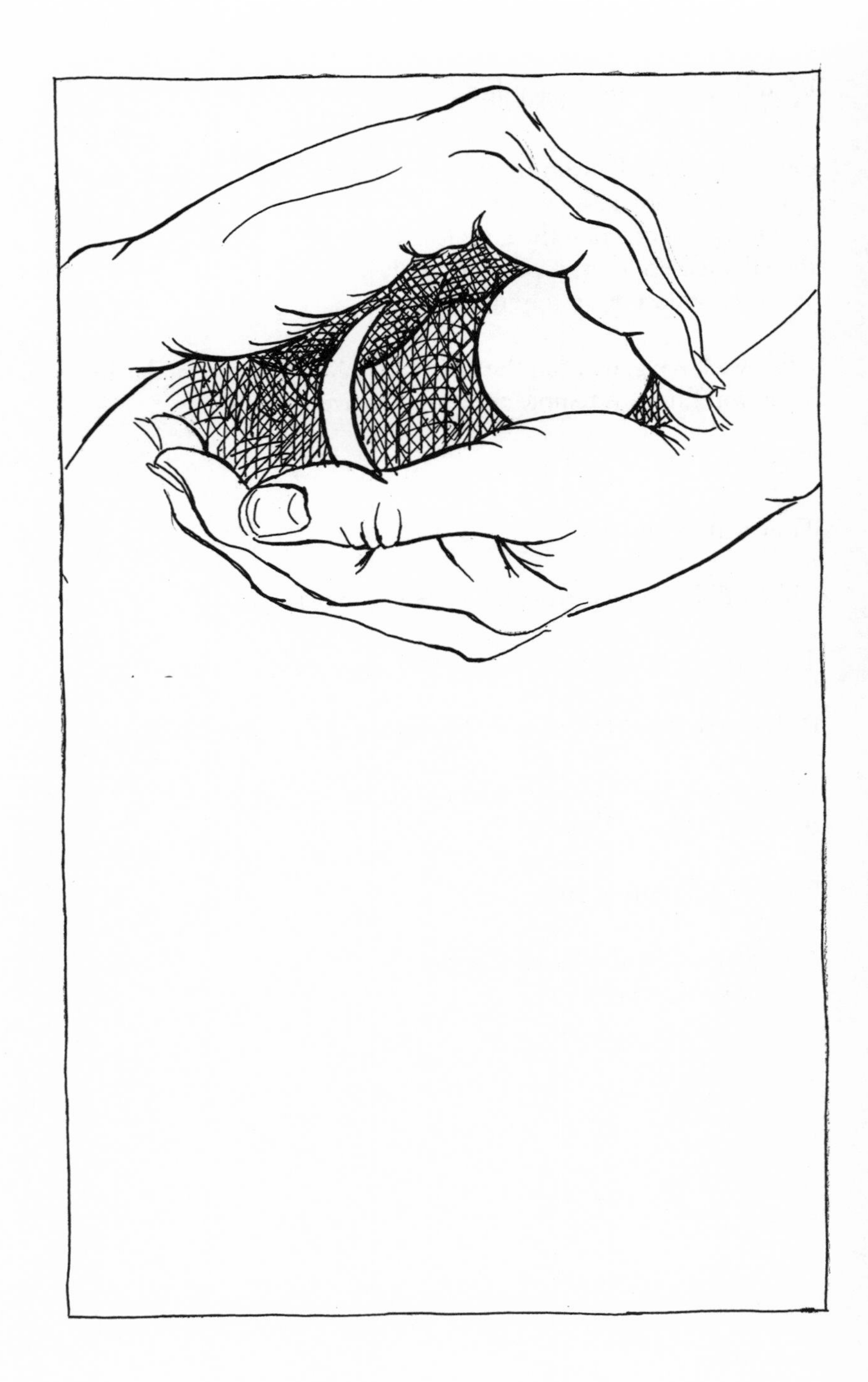

How the Moon Came to Be

In the beginning a giant god held the horizon
cupped in his hands.
When he opened them, it was day;
when he closed them, it was night.
Once this giant did not open his hands for a thousand years.
The gods were upset but did nothing
until a god who had never seen the giant
flew through a crack in the sky
and crawled out between his fingers.
She found him sitting on a stone,
barely able to keep his eyes open.

You are tired, she said. Why don't you rest?

I am holding a horizon in my hands, he replied.
I cannot put it down.

Why not? asked the god.

If I put it down, it will grow cold, answered the giant.

If you keep it locked away in your hands,
it will die of darkness, said the god.

What am I to do? asked the weary giant.

I will join you, said the god.
Then while I sleep, you can hold the horizon in your hands,
and while you sleep, I can hold it in mine.

And that is how the moon came to be
and why the sun shares his light with her.

How Clouds Came to Be

In the days when the sun and the moon were lovers,
they rose and fell like two boats on a tide.

An envious god said to the sun,
You are not so pleasant to look upon as your lover.
She is silver and fair while you are red and ugly.
Is it any wonder those who look at you turn away?

The angry sun burst into flames.
The moon, unable to bear the flames, fled.

The man in the moon is the reflection of the sun's face
in her own as she gazes at him
from the dark side of the Earth.

The clouds in the sky are tears that fall from her eyes.

And the wind that blows them
from one end of the Earth to the other?
That is the envious god sighing.

How the Tides Came to Be

Once a river swallowed a god. Here is how it happened.
When gods walked along the horizon,
one among them wanted to fly.
She tried leaping from boulders and trees and hillocks,
but she always fell straight to earth.
One day, desperate, she tried jumping from a cliff
and fell into a river far below.

What have you done? asked the river
as it flowed past her broken body.

I wanted to fly, sighed the god as she died.

In the fall turtles and eels stripped the flesh from her bones.
In the spring spawning salmon nibbled at her eyes.

When there was nothing left except the river itself,
the river said,
Now that I have swallowed a god, I am surely become one,
and ran as fast as it could to the ocean.

Make way for a god, said the river.

But the ocean did not listen, and when the river rushed on,
the ocean swallowed it
just as surely as the river had swallowed the god.

Now I am a god, thought the ocean. I shall swallow the Earth.

And that is how waves came to be
and why they beat constantly against the shore.

The Tree of Worlds

In the beginning all the worlds grew on trees like apples
and the gods picked them as they pleased.
One day a god, her fingers white as the Milky Way,
reached for the Earth,
but a shining god reached out as well,
and when their hands touched,
the Earth slipped through her fingers.

My world has fallen through the sky, said the first god.
I'll never find it again.

It was a puny world, said the shining god.

Then why did you reach for it?

I didn't, said the shining god.
I was reaching for this instead.

He plucked a plump, shiny world
growing next to where the Earth had been,
and he took a bite.

This is a tasty world, he said, offering her a bite.

She shook her head.
I prefer mine, she said,
and off she went in search of the Earth.

And that is why the Earth is still alive and why some say
that if the pale-fingered god should ever find us,
we will disappear.

Why a God Sat Motionless on the Horizon

Once a god the size of a mountain sat on the horizon,
and though he was not made of stone, his head never turned.

The other gods were displeased.
He neither spoke nor looked at them
but stared straight ahead.
So, from a place behind the sun,
the other gods hurled trees big as hills,
rivers wide as continents,
but they could not budge this god from his place.

One day a bird, black with a red tear beneath each eye,
flew across the horizon and sat on the shoulder of this god.

Why do you never look to the left or the right? asked the bird.

I see Death ahead of me, the god answered,
and I am afraid that if I take my eyes off him,
he will come upon me unexpectedly.

But if you do nothing except await your fate,
your fate is already upon you, said the bird.

The god turned his head to answer,
but just as he did,
a boulder the size of a valley struck him on his temple,
killing him.

And that is how even the wisest of words can hurt
more than they help.

How Birds Began to Sing

In the beginning, birds flew letters against the clouds
and punctuated branches at night.
But they would not sing.

Every morning an anxious god
whistled beneath the trees, to no avail.
The sound of wind under wings was their only sound.

One day a bird the god had never seen before
settled atop a mountain.
At night it sang like the moon on a pond,
at dawn like the sunrise across the horizon,
and though it lived a thousand years,
a morning came when the anxious god found it
shrouded by its own wings.

After I am dead, said the bird,
take out my breast bone and carve a flute from it.
When you play it, the others will sing.

But the god would not wait.
She tore open its breast and sucked the marrow from its bone,
made holes along the edges and, raising it to her lips,
blew the silence after rain.
That morning the birds began to sing.

And that is why there is an ache in one's heart
when a bird sings and when it does not.

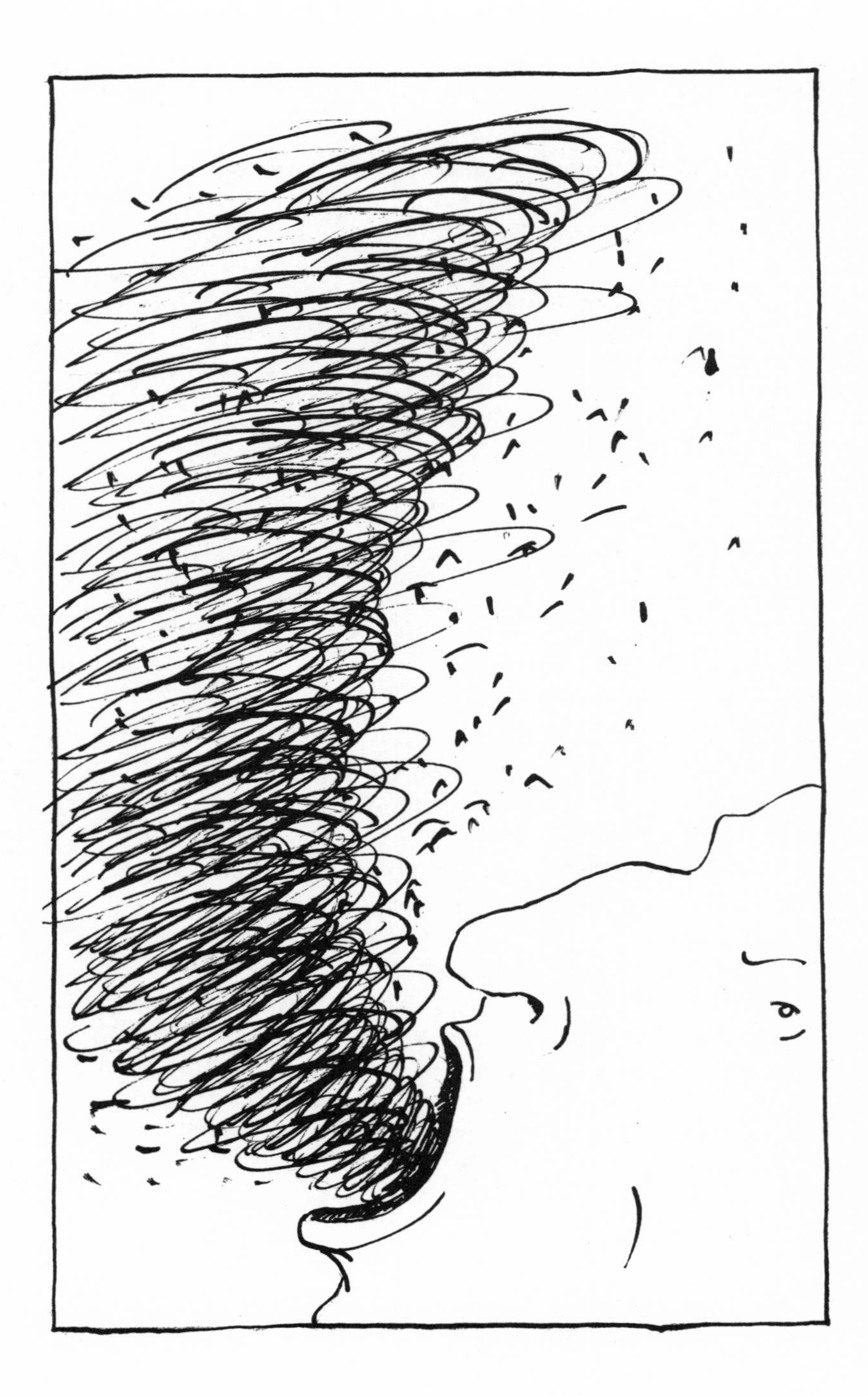

How a God Met the Black Wind

One day a god watched as a black wind whirled
across the horizon, sucking up everything in its path.

Stop, said the god. You are destroying the horizon.
Soon there will be no difference between earth and sky.
We will have no place to walk.
People will have no place to look for us.

It is in my nature to destroy, said the wind.
I shall do the same to you if you do not step aside.

With that the black wind hurled itself upon the god,
but the god did not step aside.
Instead he opened his mouth wide and swallowed the wind
and held his breath until it stopped thrashing inside him.
Then he slowly let out his breath.
A tiny puff of air crept out of his mouth
and beat gently against the surface of a nearby pond.
Then the pond turned to glass again.

And that is why every wind ends in silence.

35 How a God Brought Peace into the World

Once an ancient god was walking along the horizon.
He came upon two gods fighting.

Why are you fighting? asked the ancient god.

I caught him swimming in my lake, said one of the fighting gods.
He didn't ask for my permission.

His lake is on my mountain, said the other god.
I don't need permission.

So what do you want him to do?
said the ancient god to the god of the lake.

I want him to take away his mountain.

And you? said the ancient god to the god of the mountain.

Let him take away his lake.

To the god of the mountain the ancient god said,
If he takes away his lake, you will have nowhere to swim.
And to the god of the lake he said,
If he takes away his mountain,
you will have no place for your lake.

What shall we do? asked the fighting gods.

If each of you gives to the other what is yours,
then you will each have what you want.

And that is how it is possible to keep something by giving it away.

The Tortoise

Once there was a very old god who had been sitting
on a rock by the sea for as long as she could remember,
shaking her head from side to side,
moaning in time to the waves.

One night a tortoise as ancient as the god
crawled out of the water
and dragged itself to the rock,
its mottled shell glistening in the moonlight.

Why do you shake your head and moan so? asked the tortoise.

I want to die, said the ancient god, but Death does not come.

If he does not come to you, you must go to him.

Where does Death live?

Climb on my back and I will show you.

With the ancient god clinging to its shell,
the tortoise lumbered into the sea and swam for seven nights
beyond the horizon.

On the seventh night it said, Here is where Death lives.
And it slid beneath the waves,
leaving the ancient god to drown.

And that is how Death comes in his own time
and why waiting for him is a waste of ours.

37 |

The Frightened God

When the gods first opened their eyes
and found themselves alone in a world they had not made,
they were afraid to move.

I will be afraid for all of you, said one of the gods,
so that you can go out into the world free of fear.
All I ask is that you return and tell me what it is like.

And so the gods walked out along the horizon
and found the trees and the mountains and the brooks.
They made birds and flowers and fish and gave color to everything.
Caught up in the beauty of all they had done,
they forgot the god who was afraid for them
until, after a thousand years, they chanced upon her,
grown old and shriveled, her eyes yellow with terror.
The gods rushed to embrace her,
and when they touched her, terror spread over each of them.

Now it is your turn to be afraid for me,
said the god, no longer fearful.

And she walked out along the horizon to see the world,
leaving the others huddled together,
staring in terror at the stars.

And that is why freedom and fear are constant companions.

The Circle of Gods

Toward the end only seven gods remained.
Although they loved one another,
they were lonely for those who were gone.

One said, There should be more of us.

It is all we can do to keep ourselves alive, said a second.

We need more gods, insisted a third.

Before it is too late, said a fourth.

It is already too late, said a fifth.

It is never too late, said a sixth.

We shall see, said the seventh god. Join hands and form a circle.

When they had formed the circle,
a new god suddenly stood in their midst.
No sooner had the new god joined than another god appeared
and another and another
until the Earth was teeming with gods.

Stop, said the first god. Soon there will be no room for us.

The seventh god threw down his hands.
The multitude of gods vanished,
leaving the seven gods alone again,
their hands at their sides.

We shall miss them, said one god.

Yes, said another. It would have been better if they had never come.

And that is why it is often better to want what you cannot have
than to have what you cannot keep.

Why the Gods Left No Trace When They Died

Even as the gods walked the horizon,
they knew that people would come after they had left,
and so they considered how to let them know
that gods had preceded them.

We could carve our names into rock, said one god.

They would think their ancestors had done it, said another.

We could raise an edifice so intricate they would know
only gods could have done such a thing, said a third.

It would frighten them, said another god.
They would tear it down when they came upon it.

If we leave no trace at all, perhaps they will make us up,
suggested another.

And so the gods removed every trace
of their ever having walked the horizon.
They silenced the birds,
stopped the clouds in their tracks,
rolled the sun and the moon into a single ball,
put the sea to rest,
drained the color from the Earth.

When they had finished, a god said,
We are leaving behind a dismal place.

Perhaps, said another god, it is better to leave our works.

And that is why the world is beautiful
and the gods forgotten.

Why the Gods Were Left Behind

In the beginning the horizon teemed with gods,
but with each passing eon one less god stood on the horizon
until there were only seven,
each sitting atop an ancient stone, lamenting.

Now that the others have gone, they each thought to themselves,
why are we left behind?

Perhaps it is a punishment, said the first god.

Or a reward, said the second.

Perhaps we are forgotten, said the third.

Who would have forgotten us? said the fourth.

Our ancestors, said the fifth.

We have no ancestors, said the sixth.

If we want to leave the Earth, said the seventh god,
perhaps we must first forget one another.

And so the gods embraced the stones they sat upon
as if they were lovers. They spoke softly to the stones
and caressed their blemishes
and loved them so deeply that they soon forgot the other gods.
But stone is only stone, and because it cannot love in return,
the gods grew even more desolate
and in their desolation remembered one another.

And that is why you can forget yourself
only if what you love loves you.

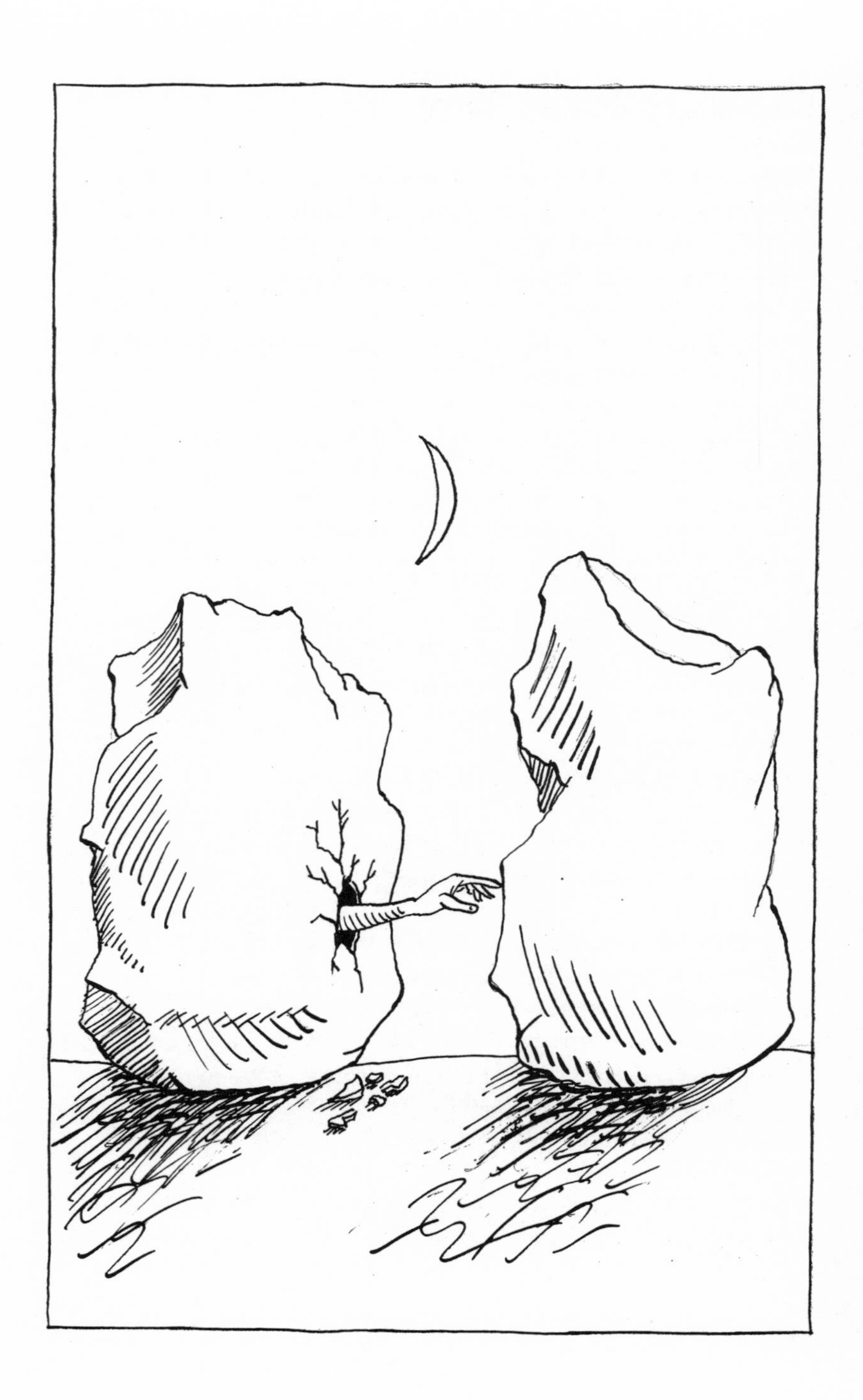

The Stony Gods

As the gods grew older, they each held on to their own wrists
or sat on the horizon, their chins resting on their knees,
their arms wound around their legs or crossed over their chests.
Before, they walked arm in arm, sometimes four abreast.
Now they touched only themselves.

One day a boulder tumbled from the side of a mountain
and came to rest in the center of the circle of gods.
Awakened from their reverie, they came, one by one,
to where the boulder was, and touched it.

Why is it that we touch a stone but not one another? asked a god.

Because, said a second god, stones ask nothing in return.

The other gods began to speak.

And why do we touch only ourselves?

Because, like stones, we ask nothing of ourselves.

And why do we ask nothing of ourselves?

Perhaps because we have nothing to give.

Nonsense, said the seventh god. This stone has no life.
Even so it has given to us.

And that is why only by touching others do we touch ourselves.

How the Gods Learned to Die

When the gods were so old they could not walk,
they sat in a circle facing outward on the horizon
so that each saw a different thing—
a boulder, a hillock, a tree with a blackbird at the top,
a wave breaking, a mulberry bush, a cloud.

My legs are like tree trunks, said the first god.

My eyes are like stone, said the second.

My tongue is like ice, said the third.

My fingernails are like seashells, said the fourth.

It is time for us, said the fifth.

The sixth god, facing outward so that he looked at a cloud, said,
Let us be what we see and let what we see be us.

But that has always been so, said the seventh god.

And so the gods sat still on the horizon, in a circle,
facing outward, looking at themselves.

And that is why, when the gods close their eyes,
the world will disappear.

43 | # The Origin of Life

At first the gods walked hundreds abreast
in columns that filled the horizon
until one day a single god turned
and walked another way.
A second god followed suit, and then a third,
and soon the gods were walking
in as many different directions as there were gods,
and the horizon was empty.

Seeing that he was alone, an ancient god lay down
in the middle of the horizon
and stayed there for a thousand years.
One day a young god found him there.

What are you doing? asked the young god.

Once, said the ancient god, you and I
might have walked as companions do, arm in arm.
But one of us turned round, and then another,
and now we are as far from one another
as one end of the universe is from the other.

And so the young god lay down next to the elder,
and soon a third god joined them, and a fourth, and after a time
the horizon was once again filled with thousands of gods
lying in droves along the way.

And that is how the first universe ended.